This book belongs to:

~~LOKI~~

Vaelan Tamijmarane

6 sandelwood avenue

I am a reader and I celebrated
World Book Day 2024 with this gift from
my local bookseller and Walker Books.

IV2 6GR

World Book Day's mission is to offer every child and young person the opportunity to read and love books by giving you the chance to have a book of your own. To find out more, and for fun activities including video stories, audiobooks and book recommendations, visit worldbookday.com. World Book Day is a charity sponsored by National Book Tokens.

This book is dedicated to Gus – the mighty god child

First published 2024 by Walker Books Ltd
87 Vauxhall Walk, London SE11 5HJ

2 4 6 8 10 9 7 5 3 1

© 2024 Louie Stowell

The right of Louie Stowell to be identified as author of this work has been asserted in accordance with the Copyright, Designs and Patents Act 1988

World Book Day® and the associated logo are the registered trademarks of World Book Day® Limited. Registered charity number 1079257 (England and Wales). Registered company number 03783095 (UK).

This book has been typeset in Autumn Voyage, Neato Serif Rough, Open Sans, WB Loki and WT Mediaeval

Printed and bound by CPI Group (UK) Ltd, Croydon CR0 4YY

British Library Cataloguing in Publication Data: a catalogue record for this book is available from the British Library

ISBN 978-1-5295-1972-3

www.walker.co.uk

WALKER
BOOKS

MIX
Paper | Supporting
responsible forestry
FSC® C014496

LOUIE STOWELL

LOKI

TALES OF
A BAD GOD

About this book:

Welcome to the glorious pages of my mortal diary. It is I, Loki, condemned to live in the form of a mortal child as punishment for my so-called crimes in Asgard.

Very cool adult me with amazing hair

Mortal child me with slightly less cool (but still very cool) hair

I am sure you have already heard of me, given how fabulous I am. But for any out there who have somehow missed the good news that is ME, I shall catch you up...

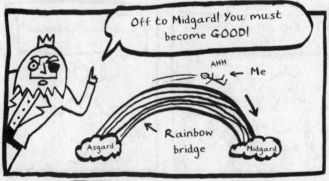

On Midgard (or "Earth") I gained a new family.

 Heimdall (Fake dad)

 Hyrrokkin (Fake mum)

Thor aka "Thomas" (Fake brother)

Fido (Fake dog — real wolf)

I also made some friends.

 Valerie

Georgina

And some enemies.

 GRR

Frost Giant

As to being good?

Thor's toothbrush

Toilet →

That's a work in progress.

Now you're all caught up, let's embark
on new adventures. They will be very brave
and noble.

> **That remains to be seen.**   !

I should also point out that this diary is
magical and detects lies. If I stray even a crisp's
width away from the truth, it corrects me. And
sometimes, it interrupts me just to be snarky.

> **Lie detected: I am a simulation of the
> Great and Dignified God Odin himself!**   !
> **I am never just "snarky".**

> **Well, maybe once or twice. When
> necessary.**   !

Day One:
Friday

LOKI VIRTUE SCORE OR LVS:

Reset for fresh start (again).

Today, I returned home from school ready for the sweet release of the weekend, only to learn tragic, terrible news!

> ! Oh no! What happened? Has someone been hurt?

Worse.

> ! Has someone died???

Even worse.

Oh, it is so, *so* much worse than that.

I have purchased a new parenting book!

How To Make Your Foul Spawn Successful (Unlike You)

By An Actually Successful Dad

Every time Heimdall buys a parenting book, he inevitably tries to inflict new forms of torture upon me. Sure enough, as he showed me this latest literary monstrosity he declared, "Things are going to change around here! No more Mr Nice God. It's tough love only!"

You were being nice BEFORE?

GO TO YOUR ROOM!

That was no problem. My room is where my phone is, which is where my games live. And the internet. And my video compilation of Thor falling over set to dramatic music. My phone is truly an infinite palace of wonders. I began to trot upstairs quite happily...

After an interminable phoneless hour, Heimdall summoned me back downstairs for further torture in Thor's company.

"My book recommends fostering a spirit of healthy competition between siblings," said Heimdall. "Pitting a weaker child..." He pointed (inexplicably) to me. "...against a stronger one..." At this he pointed (equally inexplicably) to Thor. "...encourages them to be *less* pathetic."

I do not know where Heimdall gets his book recommendations, but it cannot be a nice place.

"Therefore, I shall set a quest in the form of three challenges."

"Hurrah!" Thor cried, full of idiotic joy.

"Turds!" I cried, full of disgusted horror.

I let out the deep, world-weary sigh of one who has seen it all, done it all and suffered it all.

"Very well. What are these challenges?"

"I will begin by giving you both a present," said Heimdall.

 Now that sounded promising. How bad could a challenge be if it began with a present? Perhaps the present was a pony and the challenge was to brush its silky, silky mane? Or plait its swishing tail? That would be no trouble at all. I have helped Valerie with her plaits before.

! **I am not sure HELP is the right word...**

Heimdall led us out to the garden, my heart soaring in hope of a pony ... only for it to plummet on seeing two mortal contraptions known as bicycles.

12

Bicycle: a mode of transport used by mortals that has two wheels and (usually) no engine. They are also famously hard to draw.

Makes no sense as a device to carry a person

Does not stand up on its own

Narrow wheels

As presents go, this was profoundly disappointing.

"Why did you buy us these absurd objects?" I asked.

"You must learn how to learn to ride them!" said Heimdall, beaming. "The first of you to achieve this relatively modest feat will win the first round of the competition!"

Thor seized the handlebars of his bike with all the enthusiasm he usually reserves for slaying giants or farting on my head.

"This will be both easy and enjoyable!" He pushed the bicycle down past the side of the house and out into the street, whistling happily.

I took my bike more gingerly, as though it might explode in my hands. "How in Odin's name am I supposed to get it to remain upright while I am sitting on it? Magic?"

No! Using magic would be cheating!

I sighed so deeply that my daughter Hel (who lives in a realm deep beneath the earth) probably heard it. Incidentally, her realm is also called Hel. It gets Hel-a confusing.

"Go on, then," said Heimdall, shooing me after Thor.

"What if I fall?" I asked. "My mortal form is easily damaged, and I suspect if I break this one, Odin will not give me another lightly."

Hel

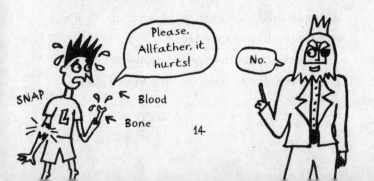

Please, Allfather, it hurts!

No.

SNAP

Blood

Bone

14

"My book says that you have to take risks in order to grow," said Heimdall.

I was beginning to think that Heimdall's book was at serious risk of a mysterious accident involving a hungry goat.

(Goats eat ANYTHING. As I have learned to my great sorrow, after leaving my favourite trousers in munching range of the goats that pull Thor's chariot.)

Despite my fear for the safety of my limbs, I bravely pushed the bike out into the road. Heimdall followed me. We were just in time to see Thor, already pedalling his bicycle and whooping in triumph.

WAHOO!

Round one to Thor.

"Perhaps you will have more luck tomorrow with round two?" said Heimdall, patting me on the shoulder.

I let out a hiss. The sort of hiss that a very gracious loser might emit.

> **!** It was the hiss of a very sore loser, who lost, losingly.

Well, *I* had cleverly avoided damaging any of my blessed limbs, while Thor now has a cut on his knee from falling off the cursed bicycle on one of his first attempts.

So, in truth, I was the winner.

> **!** ... sure.

Day Two:
Saturday

For the next challenge, Heimdall took us to the local playground. It was swarming with children and their attendant adults, and my heart lifted a little. Perhaps our challenge would be the less heinous task of taking turns on the roundabout and whomever was sick first, lost?

Sick bag

I had not eaten much at lunch, for it contained suspicious mystery meat, so I fancied my chances. Alas, Heimdall took us past the roundabout to point out a mortal girl – Coat Girl from school. She's in the year below us and she always wears a big puffy, pink coat. She is very proud of how big, puffy and pink it is.

TREMBLE BEFORE MY MIGHTY COAT!

"Your second challenge is to get that girl to remove her coat," said Heimdall.

"Is it valuable?" asked Thor.

"No," said Heimdall.

"Magical?"

"No."

"Is it—"

"Let me stop you there." Heimdall looked weary of Thor's questions. "The point is not to possess the coat. The point is that it will be immensely difficult to pry the coat from the child's form."

"How do you know about Coat Girl?" I was surprised he had any knowledge of the young mortals at my school.

"From the parents' chat group of course!" said Heimdall, brandishing his phone.

I felt momentarily sad that he was in a chat group other than our family one. But then I remembered that I think the "family" chat is a pitiful charade. They're not even my real family.

18

Methinks the diary doth be deluded.

"The mother is desperate to clean the coat," Heimdall said, "but the daughter refuses to remove it even when she is asleep. Thus, the coat will be immensely difficult to obtain!"

MotheroftheCoatedOne:

I tried to wash it last night and she climbed inside the washing machine screaming "I WILL NEVER FORGIVE YOU, MOTHER! I AM GOING TO LIVE IN HERE UNTIL YOU SWEAR TO LEAVE MY COAT ALONE."

TheParentHyrrokkinHates:

Please sign my petition against eggs in school. Eggs are unhygienic.

"So," said Heimdall. "The first of you to persuade her to cast off the coat shall win this round! I shall wait here and observe as you make your attempts." And he went to join the group of adults watching their spawn playing on the swings and other playground items.

Thor bounded straight up to Coat Girl.

At least *some* mortals are immune to Thor's doltish charms. He walked back over to me and slumped down on a tree stump. "I fear this challenge is impossible. I cannot resort to violence, for that would not be noble against such a small opponent, and I have tried asking politely. What else is there?"

"What else indeed..." I said. I feared that even my vast stores of natural charm and charisma would not be enough. Coat Girl had a steely look about her that suggested words alone would fail. And I, of course, would never consider resorting to violence.

Because you are an abject coward who fears all forms of physical conflict? !

> No! Because she's smaller and younger than me and it would be wrong!

And? !

> And because I am an abject coward who fears all forms of physical conflict.

But I am not without other talents. Many, many other talents. The cogs of my brilliant mind began to whir.

21

A plan was forming. A plan of such genius that even Odin would be astounded.

But, for my inspired plan to succeed, I would need funds. Funds, bait, and a secret weapon. First, the funds...

Please may I have some money to buy food?

I raised my voice to make sure the other adults could hear. "My friend was just saying what a cruel father you are, but I told them they were wrong and that you are in fact generous and kind. Please may I have some money?"

Heimdall narrowed his eyes, but reluctantly handed over a note.

"Very well," he grunted. "But no crisps."

"I promise I will not buy crisps," I agreed.

Now for the bait. If there was one thing I knew about Coat Girl, it was that she loves her coat.

But if there were two things I knew about her, it was that she also loves dogs, having witnessed a heated playground argument between her and Valerie as to which animal is best: horse or dog?

There were many dogs in the park, but what I needed was for there to be one in the café... Fortunately there were many.

A weak-minded mortal who liked dogs may consider all of these dogs to be cute. I am of course immune to their charms, but— OMG SHE LICKED MY FACE SO CUTE!

Finally, I had to sneak home to quickly retrieve my secret weapon. As our house is located near the park – and I am a master of stealth and agility – I was able to get back without anyone noticing.

Once I'd positioned my secret weapon in the right place inside the café (near a particularly cute and fluffy dog) it was time to secure my target.

Excited squealing noises

Once Coat Girl had calmed herself, I took her to the café. For my plan to work, I needed Coat Girl to remain in the café for longer than it took to simply admire a dog. Time for phase two.

"Can I buy you some cake?" I asked her.

She nodded, clearly awed by my incredible generosity. For Coat Girl I bought a cake with lots of oozing jam that looked fiddly to eat, and some chips for me.

(See? I kept my oath to Heimdall and did not buy any crisps.)

> ! While this is true, you know in your heart that substituting one form of banned fried potatoes for another form of fried potatoes is not acceptable behaviour.

I realized that I needed to ensure I had a witness for my imminent triumph. I excused myself without waiting for her to finish her mouthful of cake, then rushed to the bench where Thor was sulking beside Heimdall.

"Come and see for yourself..." I said with a mysterious smile, ignoring a sudden surge of terror that my plan might, in that very public moment, fail.

To my great joy, on returning to the café, we beheld Coat Girl. Coatless at last.

She was looking relieved – and much, much cooler.

"Patience," I said, shaking my head.

"You threatened her with patience?!" Thor said in confusion.

"No, YOU be patient, trollwit!" I hissed.
"I will explain later."

When Coat Girl got up and left, waving goodbye and picking up her coat again, I took the others to the table she had vacated.

Then I unplugged the spare electric heater I'd borrowed from home and handed it to Heimdall with a flourish. "Ta da!"

"Very clever. Round two goes to you."

Thor grumbled. "That isn't fair. I didn't know we were allowed to use equipment!"

"No," said Heimdall. "But if you weren't sure, then you should have asked."

I gave Thor an enormous smug smile. "Not so wonderful at this game *now* are you, Mr Pedals?"

Thor sulked for the entire evening. Unfortunately, that meant a thunderstorm formed over our house. But it *did* mean that Thor got into trouble.

Stop that right now! If lightning strikes my petunias, Loki wins by default!

Day Three:
Sunday

After breakfast, Heimdall took us upstairs.

In your bedrooms you will find everything you need to complete your third and final challenge.

This gave me hope that the challenge might be "who can take the longest nap" but sadly, that was not to be. What awaited was a lot of pieces of wood, screws and mysterious bits of plastic, plus roughly half of the contents of Hyrrokkin's toolbox.

"It's a wardrobe," said Heimdall. "Thor has one too. Whoever builds theirs first, wins."

"That," I said, pointing to the chaos littering the carpet, "is not a wardrobe. It is a mess."

28

"Here are the instructions," Heimdall said, ignoring my very good point and handing me a piece of paper covered in various diagrams which supposedly showed how to turn the pile of rubbish on my floor into a wardrobe.

I peered at it. It didn't look *too* difficult for a genius like me. But there was one problem: I am not the handiest with a hammer. Nor am I strong enough to lift things like the larger parts of an unmade wardrobe.

After a while I grew bored of failing and went to see how Thor was getting on. I was pleased to discover he had not started constructing the wardrobe either.

I don't understand these. What do I need to hit with a hammer?

It was at this moment that I remembered something important. Heimdall wanted us to do what he said like good little mortals. But I am not a good little mortal. I am a rulebreaker. A world-shaker. A troublemaker. I didn't have to do things his way!

"Dear 'brother', I would like to propose an alliance," I said.

Thor just looked confused.

"I mean, we should team up against Heimdall," I explained.

"I know what an alliance means," said Thor. "It's a war word. But why would you want one?"

He thinks he has set us an impossible task. But I am a trickster and nothing is impossible! I wish to prove him very, very wrong!

But if we work together, that means we will tie and neither of us will win. In a competition, one person must have victory, or it is not a competition.

"But Heimdall will *lose*, granting victory to us both," I said. "Or you can stand there looking confused and we'll both get very bored." I gestured to the pieces of wood. "I can't lift half of those!"

Thor looked unsure. But then he looked at the instructions again. While he could lift heavy things with his muscly arms, his brain was NOT capable of any heavy-lifting.

"OK," he said.

So, I read the instructions and Thor put the pieces together under my calm and wise supervision.

Although I gave beautifully clear instructions, Thor made many errors.

Correction: Not only did you give many unclear instructions, you also used some words to describe Thor's performance that will DEFINITELY lose you virtue points.

What matters is that, eventually, we were done. I gave the wardrobe a little prod, and it did not fall to pieces. Considering that its pieces were not exactly hewn out of the finest trees in the Nine Realms, I considered this to be a good outcome.

"Heimdall, we're ready!" I called.

He came in and observed the wardrobe.

"Very nice. Which one of you made it?" he asked.

Thor hung his head in shame. "We failed, Heimdall. Neither of us could build it alone so we had to share the task. I am sorry. This is a deep humiliation."

"So," said Heimdall, looking very serious. "You are saying that instead of competing against one another, each used his own skills to help the other, and you worked together to achieve something that many mortals cannot do without screams of wrath?"

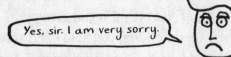

Yes, sir. I am very sorry.

I watched Heimdall's stern frown transform into a beaming smile and in that moment, I knew I had been played.

You WANTED us to work together, didn't you?

32

Heimdall waggled his eyebrows at us with an irritatingly mysterious and Odinic smile.

"Well done, boys," he said.

As he left the room, he held his book close, gazing upon it with the fondness of a father seeing his newborn child for the first time.

"So," said Thor. "The great Loki, god of tricksters, got tricked. And not by Odin or another trickster ... but by honest Heimdall." He slapped me on my shoulder. "I think you're losing your touch, my little chaos goblin of a fake brother."

"You got tricked too," I grumbled as I rubbed my sore shoulder.

Thor shrugged. "I don't care about being tricked. We built a wardrobe together! As a team! That brings me joy!"

"Well, us working together does remind me of *another* time we worked as a team," I said. Thor looked baffled, so I continued, "That time with Thrym..."

Thor blushed.

"Come to think of it," I went on, "I feel Valerie and Georgina should know of it."

"NO!" said Thor. "Not THAT story. You are forbidden from telling them THAT story!"

"Oh really?" I said. "Just watch me..."

MWAHA HA HA HA HA

Day Four:
Monday

Obediently?
TAKE THAT BACK!

At lunch, Valerie and Georgina were talking about the school play where the two princesses got married at the end. The perfect opportunity to tell my tale.

For posterity's sake, I shall record the story in this diary.

The Time Thor Nearly Married a Giant
by me, Loki

It all began one glorious morning in Asgard.

> LOKI! MY HAMMER! IT HAS GONE!

"I didn't take it!" I said quickly, before he got any violent ideas.

You see, Thor feels the same way about that hammer as mortals do about their mobile telephones – it's like an extension of his stupid, muscular body.

Luckily, I was fairly sure that a giant called Thrym was the culprit. Mostly because this had happened recently:

Now, I often find that the best way to solve a problem is to make it somebody else's. In this instance: Freyja's. (Freyja is the god of love, war and magic, among other things too numerous to write out here without my mortal hand falling off.)

Although Thor *does* always think it's giants, that doesn't mean that it's *never* giants. The Frost Giants are our sworn enemies, after all. Well, Thor's ... and Odin's. I tend to keep out of it if I can.

"Actually, on this occasion I happen to know it *is* giants," I said. "Or rather: giant. Singular. Thrym, specifically."

"Oh, him," Freyja said. "Very well. What do you two want me to do about it? I don't have time for a quest."

There are some very complicated wars happening down on Midgard that I'm overseeing.

"I wish to borrow your feather cloak!" Thor said. "So that I might fly to Jotunheim to get my hammer back."

"My cloak? Of course," said Freyja, looking relieved. Now she knew she wasn't actually going to have to do anything, she was very helpful. "Please, take it. I'd give it to you even if it was made of gold! Even if it was made of silver!"

"If it was made of gold, it would be too heavy to fly," said Thor, who doesn't really understand poetic language. Unless the poem is about farting.

The mission requires someone tactful. Moi, not that giant prune.

Thor just grunted. He didn't seem to mind me taking over the mission since it involved talking rather than hitting people with hammers. Now, normally I would have just flown in bird form to Jotunheim ... but I look *so good* in Freyja's cloak.

Mirror, mirror on the wall, who's the prettiest god of all?

After a very pleasant hour admiring myself, I flapped off to Jotunheim, where I soon found Thrym outside his grand hall. He's kind of a big deal in giant land – a king, I believe, although every other person in Jotunheim seems to be some sort of ruler or other. Personally, I think it cheapens the monarchy.

"Bad news, I'm afraid," I said, landing a safe distance away. "Someone's stolen Thor's hammer. Now, how can I put this tactfully..." I decided that perhaps an additional step away from the giant and his meaty fists would be wise. "Might you have, possibly, accidentally..." I got ready to fly away at the first sign of violence. "...taken it?"

Thrym just laughed. "I stole it, yes. And I've hidden it eight miles underground where no one will find it. Not even you, trickster."

"OK," I said, cautiously. "And... How would you feel about returning it?"

"Give it back so that Thor can beat me and my friends up with it?" said Thrym, grumpily. "I would feel bad about that."

"Right. What about a trade?" I suggested. "Anything you want! Unless it belongs to me, obviously. And definitely not this fabulous cloak." I pulled it closer around me, to make a point of how good I looked in it.

I don't want your stupid cloak. I want a wife!

I'm flattered, really. My female forms are very beautiful, but I'm dating the goddess Sigyn AND a giant called Angrboda, so my dance card is rather full...

"Not you," Thrym growled. "I want Freyja as my wife. She is the most beautiful."

Well, that hurt my feelings, but I promised Thrym to do what I could, and flew away, leaving the giant whistling what sounded like "Here comes the bride".

4-2

Thor immediately fell into a sulk, until I told him Thrym would return his hammer if Freyja agreed to marry the giant.

"What are we waiting for then?" said Thor.

> Wait, you can't just—

Too late. He'd already just.

By the time I arrived at Freyja's hall, Thor was barking out orders. "Quick! Freyja! Put on a wedding dress! You have to marry Thrym or he won't give my hammer back!"

"Thor!" I hissed.

Freyja wasn't just angry. She was FURIOUS. She was so furious her neck bulged and her necklace pinged off.

"This isn't *Midgard*!" she yelled. "You can't go around promising to marry me to people! I'm a god, not a piece of property!"

"Speaking of property..." I handed Freyja her cloak. "Yours, I believe. Thank you so much, ever so grateful..."

Then I made a diplomatic exit and left Thor to get shouted at.

Soon, Ratatosk appeared in my chambers. It seemed Odin had heard the news. Not surprising, given that he has access to stores of knowledge most mortals could barely even comprehend.

Also, he's really nosy.

Your presence is requested immediately in the wondrous Valhalla, for an All-Asgard meeting to discuss the matter of Thor's stolen hammer, Mjolnir. We need that hammer, for Thor uses it to protect all of Asgard! The Frost Giants will only return it if Freyja agrees to marry Thrym. What shall we do?

O xx

P.S. R.S.V.P. to Ratatosk. Snacks will be provided.

P.P.S. Do not be late or I will be wrathful.

I hurried to Valhalla. Odin's lofty hall is decorated lavishly yet tastefully with many portraits and many more weapons. All the gods were gathered around the feasting table, along with Hyrrokkin, who was visiting from her cottage in the snowy woods of Jotunheim.

I have already discussed this matter with Freyja and she is very firm in her desire NOT to marry Thrym.

He's gross. I once saw him eat raw meat out of his own dog's mouth.

"So, what is our best course of action?" asked Heimdall.

"Storm Jotunheim and attack the giants with our bare hands!" shouted Thor.

GROAN

Having graciously allowed Thor – god of worthless ideas – to come up with a useless notion, I stepped in with a brilliant suggestion.

FINE. Heimdall came up with an idea.

"We should dress Thor up as Freyja, with her necklace, and a veil to cover his face," said Heimdall. "Then he can sweep into Thrym's home as his bride and catch the giant off-guard during the wedding. As soon as they bring out Mjolnir, Thor can snatch it up and..." He mimed Thor bashing a giant with his hammer.

I had to admit, it was a good plan. It wasn't the simplest, or most elegant, but it *was* the funniest. Thor is the butchest being in all of the Nine Realms, and the idea of him in a wedding gown was delightful.

 Everyone will make fun of me. You know I don't look good in a dress.

"Don't do yourself down, my love," said the goddess Sif. (His wife, who didn't seem to mind him remarrying.) "You look good in everything."

"Thor, if we are to make this plan work, you must first bathe," I observed. "I can smell you from here, and that will be a slight giveaway that you are not the most fragrant Freyja."

While Thor bathed, Freyja went and got some of her finest dresses.

A few quick magical adjustments later...

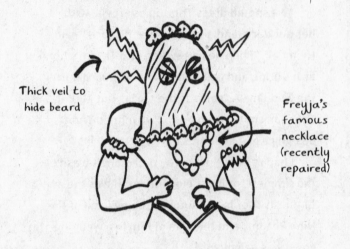

Thick veil to hide beard

Freyja's famous necklace (recently repaired)

As Thor would surely mess up this delicate mission if he went alone, I volunteered to go as his beautiful bridesmaid. I know upstaging the bride is frowned upon, but in this case it was unavoidable.

Never mind the bride, HERE COMES THE BRIDESMAID!

"Let's go!" I cried, excited to show off my outfit— I mean, achieve the object of our quest. Which was rescuing Thor's hammer.

"We can take my goat chariot!" said Thor, shifting uncomfortably in his wedding dress.

When we climbed into the chariot, I was very glad I'd made Thor bathe. Sadly, the goats had not.

Fragrant (good) →   ← Fragrant (bad)

"Let's get this over with," Thor grunted, as we set off into the sky. As he drove, he ranted at me. "This dress is incredibly itchy. The bodice is too tight! It doesn't even have pockets! I cannot believe I have to do this."

"Remember, you'll get your hammer back at the end of it," I pointed out.

"And then Thrym will get my hammer back. IN HIS HEAD," growled Thor, urging the goats on faster. In fact, we went so fast that the mountains beneath us shook and split in two. Volcanoes exploded as we passed.

Thor's parking is as bad as his driving and we set down outside Thrym's abode with a mighty THUMP.

Thrym was there to greet us, wearing his finest clothes and looking excited. "Freyja! Welcome to my incredibly vast and majestic home," he said.

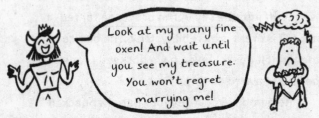

Look at my many fine oxen! And wait until you see my treasure. You won't regret marrying me!

I suspected the same would not be true for Thrym. If he lived long enough to *have* regrets, that is.

The giant took Thor by the hand and led him into his gold-plated, diamond-studded hall. Thrym's sense of style was not what you'd call subtle.

50

He sat his "beautiful" bride down at his right-hand side, while I sat on Thrym's left. As the feast began, Thor did not hold back. First, he ate a whole roast ox in a couple of bites.

Then he shovelled eight entire salmon up under his veil into his mouth.

Have you seen a whole salmon? They're *massive*.

Then he ate many (many) plates of cakes and drank three whole barrels of mead.

Thrym watched open-mouthed. "Wow. You ... do you always eat like this? Being married to you could get expensive. Not that I can't afford it," he added hastily, gesturing around his hall.

Uh-oh, I thought. If Thrym saw through the disguise before Thor laid hands on the hammer, we'd be in big trouble. Luckily, Thor's very witty, very beautiful bridesmaid was ready with an excuse.

"Ah, you see, poor Freyja was so excited to marry you that she couldn't eat a thing for..." I measured up how much Thor had eaten. "... eight days before she came! The poor thing is ravenous!"

"Eight days? But I only asked her to marry me earlier today," said Thrym, looking confused.

I gave him my prettiest smile.

But you forget — Freyja is a powerful sorcerer. She used a spell to discover who her husband was going to be.

I gave Thrym a very flirty wink. "Naturally, she was delighted to discover it would be you, but also very nervous about the wedding."

He nodded. "There is no need to be nervous, my darling. Kiss me, beloved," Thrym said, in what he clearly thought was an alluring voice. He sounded more like a mooing cow.

As Thrym leaned over for his kiss, Thor glared at him through the veil, looking at the Frost Giant with the kind of stormy fury he usually reserved for me alone. Thrym was startled.

When he'd lumbered back to the table, looking embarrassed, he turned to me and whispered, "Maiden, why are your mistress's eyes so terrifying? It looks like they're on fire with fury when they should be full of the soft light of love!"

Genius that I am, I had an answer for that too. "Our lovely Freyja was so eager for her upcoming nuptials that she didn't sleep for eight nights!"

This seemed to please Thrym.

Phew, crisis averted! Thrym was *so* pleased that he didn't ask me any more pesky questions.

> Servants, bring in Mjolnir, Thor's hammer, and I will lay it on my beautiful bride's lap! Then our wedding will be complete, as I will have fulfilled my oath to the gods!

As a servant carried in Mjolnir on a golden platter, Thrym sprang eagerly out of his seat and took it over to his "bride".

"Now I can *finally* start enjoying this party!"
Thor crowed, throwing off his veil.

THE END

"Wait!" Valerie said as I concluded my tale.

"What happened next?" asked Georgina.

"Isn't it obvious?" I leaned forward for maximum effect. "Death."

Day Five:

Tuesday

As all mortal children know, school is a cruel and
terrifying punishment that you can only escape
by becoming old. In my child form, I am not
spared this monstrous fate.

However, this afternoon, after a particularly wretched day at Child Prison, I came up with a cunning trick that would mean I could be marked as "present" on the school register while actually remaining at home and in comfort (rather than in Maths, in anguish).

> **I can already tell that this will be a bad idea.** !

I would create a robot copy of myself! It would go to school in my stead! I would play computer games all day!

> **I take it back. It's a TERRIBLE idea.** !

Obviously I would be more handsome than this, even in my robot form.

The first step in my ~~cunning trick~~ simple plan was watching many films about robots for research. In them I learned that robots are frequently:

1: Indistinguishable from mortals until they speak.

> I speak in a strange monotone because although my creator spent hours making me look realistic, they did not bother to give me any tonal variation in my speech patterns.

KILL CRUSH DESTROY!

2: Homicidal. Many robots turn into killers. (Note to self: make robot not do this, that would *not* be good for my virtue score.)

3: From the future. As I do not have access to time travel this option is not currently available.

4: Controlled by a mystical ritual known as "coding".

Coding: In mortal films, coding consists of typing numbers into a computer while drinking sugary energy drinks over a period of several hours. In real life, it consists of doing those things but every single day for a year, while crying.

My friend Georgina is the best at coding in the whole school. So I went to her house to ask her robot-making advice. Immediately.

This was a distinctly unhelpful response. I followed her inside and pressed her further while she offered me a fizzy drink. I accepted it, in case it helped with the coding. I downed it in one go and then felt incredibly ill.

"Why should I not create a robot?" I asked when I had recovered. "Is it because you fear my robot will become evil and attempt to destroy all of humanity? I promise, I will not make it do that, for I am a Good God now!"

"Hmm," said Georgina, sounding less than convinced. "It's not just that you *shouldn't* make a robot."

It's that you can't! It's impossible.

I realized there had been a misunderstanding. Mortals can be so obtuse sometimes.

"Oh, *I'm* not going to make it," I explained. "You are! In movies, a child genius who knows coding can always hack into the government mainframe or build a robot out of objects they find at home. And you *are* a child genius when it comes to coding, are you not?"

Georgina leaned in and spoke slowly, as though speaking to a small child. "Films and reality aren't the same, Loki. And, yes, I'm brilliant at coding *for an eleven year old*. But I don't even know what a government mainframe *is*."

Admittedly, neither do I. It's one of those words everyone pretends they understand to avoid looking foolish. Perhaps it is a very large climbing frame run by politicians?

"So, are you saying that you are not capable of helping me create a realistic robot?" I asked, feeling deeply disappointed.

Georgina folded her arms and gave me a look. "I'm saying you need to stop thinking movies are a good source of factual information about our world. Have you tried books? You know, the paper things with words in?"

"There's no need to be sarcastic," I said.

"No," said Georgina. "But it's fun. Now go home before my mum realizes you're here and grounds me for ever for having friends over without asking."

"I use the word very, very loosely," said Georgina, shutting the door in my face.

In spite of her rudeness, I *did* take her advice: I searched for answers in a book. My spell book, to be precise. In it, I found a spell that would allow me to create a magical double of myself. Clones are not nearly as cool as robots but still, it would be a clone of wonderful *me*, which is better than a robot double of anyone else.

Clone Loki

Robot Thor

One maths symbol I DO know because it relates to one thing being more awe-inspiring than another.

┌───┐
│ ! That symbol is NOT a measure of   │
│   "awesomeness", it is a measure of—   │
└───┘

Shh, don't ruin my doodle with FACTS.

I flipped through the book until I found a suitable spell:

HOW TO CREATE A SHADOW DOUBLE

This shadow double will fulfil every request asked of it.

Ingredients:

One (fully detached) toenail (from the person you wish to duplicate)

Snake venom (tiny drop)

Four anchovies (to taste)

1. Mix ingredients in a bowl.

2. Call out the name of the person you wish to double.

3. Using your wand, create a unique mystical sigil that you have never used for any spell before. It must be at least eight gestures long and contain at least one gesture that hurts your wrist. Perform this sigil twice. Eat the contents of the bowl.

Please do not attempt this spell unless you have thought carefully about the consequences, or you will deeply regret it.

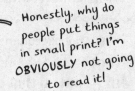

Honestly, why do people put things in small print? I'm OBVIOUSLY not going to read it!

Being a magical genius, I could easily perform the spell. Even better, the first ingredient was literally at the tips of my toes. Plus, Hyrrokkin keeps venomous snakes upstairs.

> ! **You should have read the small print...**

Just as I was gathering the ingredients, I heard a familiar, grating voice.

> It's wrong to create a double of yourself to deceive others.

I told my conscience that it wasn't deceit. It was efficient use of resources.

> ! **You told your conscience a lie, you lying liar.**

No need for name-calling, diary! I thought we were friends.

> ! **We are not friends. I am judge and jury.**

But not executioner, right?

> ! **Jury's out on that one...**

Blah, blah, blah. Let's return to the more pleasant topic of my excellent plan. It was perfect! Genius! Inspired! Brilliant!

Next, I gathered the ingredients and performed the spell. My first attempt was not hugely successful.

The second was no better. In fact, it was worse.

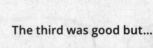

The third was good but...

Crisps? EW!

Eventually, I cracked it.

However, although it *looked* exactly like me, it was sorely lacking in my flair and genius. It just sort of stood there looking pretty. Then I remembered that it needed instructions.

"I command you to go to school in my place and pretend to be me. Make sure you behave well and do not get me into any trouble. If I'm going to get detention, I want to be able to enjoy doing the bad thing that earns me it!"

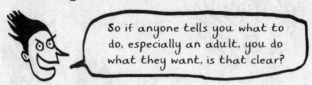

My double nodded its handsome head.

Day Six:
Wednesday

This morning, I decided to test my clone. I instructed it to go to school as normal and hid in its pocket as an ant. I was delighted with the results! In every lesson, it paid close attention and answered the teacher's questions politely and (often) accurately. It helped a fellow pupil who was upset about breaking her favourite ruler – and didn't even make fun of her for having a favourite ruler.

Can I get you anything?

No, but thank you.

! **I hope you realize you're not getting virtue points for this.**

Ah, but I'm doing my reputation among the teachers some substantial good! And it will be easier for me to behave well at school in future and gain real virtue points if all the teachers don't immediately assume I am a bucket of pus!

! **This will, as I have said before, all end in tears.**

Nonsense! The day was a great success!

Today was merely a test run, however. Tomorrow, I will send the clone to school alone so I can spend a day at home doing whatever I please!

Day Seven:
Thursday

> ## LOKI VIRTUE SCORE OR LVS:
> # 49
> **Holding steady at Not Good Enough.**

I packed the clone off to school, repeating my instructions that it should do what it was told. I then spent the morning eating crisps, relaxing in front of a television programme about people who own old things. The TV presenter tells them whether their old thing is a worthless piece of trash or, in fact, worth a considerable sum of money.

WORTHLESS TRASH!

When that grew dull, I dressed Fido up in silly costumes and posted pictures of him on the internet.

All in all, a most excellent day!

When Thor got home with the clone, I spied on them both. During dinner they were laughing and joking around, getting on like a house on fire.

All of this gave me a slightly unpleasant feeling in my stomach. But my ruse was working, so I ignored the feeling. What do feelings know?

! They know the truth that is in your heart even if not on your lying tongue.

After this disgusting display of betrayal by Thor, I made the clone hide in the wardrobe. As it was the wardrobe Thor and I made together, the structure was shoddy and risked immediate collapse, thereby crushing the clone. Well, if I was lucky.

"Get in there and behave yourself," I growled at the irritating thing.

It didn't object. In fact, it started tidying my clothes! Unnatural!

Very angry foot

I stomped downstairs to get something to eat. Heimdall came into the kitchen while I was face-deep in leftovers.

"How on Earth are you hungry again? You just ate!"

"I'm a growing boy," I pointed out.

Heimdall looked suspicious.

"Also, the meal was so delicious that I had to have seconds," I added quickly. "Your cooking is excellent!"

He gave me a big grin.

"I have to say, Loki, over the past day you've been so much better behaved and more charming than usual!"

There was that unpleasant feeling again. How could this clone be better at Loki-ing than Loki himself? How was it charming everyone?

Had I accidentally mixed in some other rogue DNA? Could it be from the loathsome Balder, god of being pleased with himself, left over from when he came to stay with us?

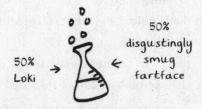

50% Loki →

← 50% disgustingly smug fartface

Day Eight:
Friday

LOKI VIRTUE SCORE OR LVS:

-451

Points removed for bunking off school and sending a clone in your place AND for humiliating poor Fido on the internet.

At breakfast, Thor, Hyrrokkin and Heimdall kept going on about how pleasant I'd been over the last two days. It made me wary of sending the clone to school again.

Were you, by any chance, starting to wonder if it was a bad idea to create a clone of yourself and allow it to roam freely through the world?

!

Don't be ridiculous. I was worried that people liked it more than they liked me.

So off the clone went to school again while I relaxed. Or tried to, at least. Every time I embarked upon a new mortal pursuit, my enjoyment was ruined by thoughts of the clone being beloved by all. When the doorbell rang around noon, I was glad of the distraction. Perhaps it would be a parcel? Parcels are an excellent mortal concept. Until you open them, they are full of limitless possibilities.

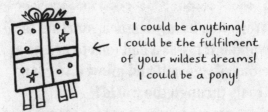

It wasn't a parcel. It was Valerie and Georgina. When I opened the door, they turned to each other and said...

THOUGHT SO!

This was not a mortal greeting with which I was familiar, but I welcomed them inside.

Something serious had to be wrong for them to leave school during the day. I had a moment of niggling horror that something might have happened to Thor. Luckily I didn't embarrass myself by asking.

"As we suspected: the you at school was fake," said Georgina, folding her arms and glaring at me.

"Look, here you are as proof," said Valerie. "There are two of you!"

"How do you know I didn't run home from school?" I said, pointing out the obvious flaw in their logic.

"When do you ever run, unless you're being chased?" said Georgina.

This was a fair point.

So, cunning mortals, you have discovered my secret. I created a clone of myself.

"I *knew* you wouldn't drop it when I said you couldn't make a robot," said Georgina with a groan.

75

"But how did you know that the me at school was fake?" I demanded. "It's a perfect copy!"

"I heard it say 'please', 'thank you' *and* 'excuse me' yesterday," said Valerie. "All in one sentence."

"And I heard it offer to help a teacher carry a heavy bag," said Georgina. "I've never seen you voluntarily carry something heavier than a burger."

I hung my head. "You knew the clone wasn't me because it was ... nice?" I asked.

"I also knew it wasn't you because it wasn't any fun," said Valerie. "I drew a picture of a horse doing a fart when we were in Maths and showed Fake Loki and it told the teacher on me!"

"But I thought everyone loved Fake Loki!" I said.

"Not me," said Valerie. "It's creepy. It doesn't have any opinions. It doesn't seem to care about anything. It just does what it's told."

Like, you're a pain, and I'm not sure I like you, but at least I don't feel bleh about you.

76

While I wasn't familiar with the mortal concept of "bleh", I got the general idea. Before I could bask in the glow of such compliments, Valerie and Georgina carried on.

That was not ideal. I checked my drawer, where I had left my wand.

Wandless

Then, I did something I had never done before. Something I never imagined I would have to do. Something I will never do again if I get any say in the matter: I ran to school.

(Except I got a stitch after five minutes and Valerie had to carry me the rest of the way.)

I thought you LIKED horses. Don't you want to know what it's like being one?

At school, although all the other pupils were eating their lunch in the hall, we found the clone alone in a corner of the playground. As we approached, it knelt down to pick up a pebble. Poking out of its pocket was my wand.

"What are you doing?" I demanded.

"Preparing a spell," said the clone. "I need a smooth pebble."

"Who told you to do a spell?" I asked.

"An adult. You told me to listen to adults,"
it said, putting the stone in its suspiciously full
pockets. "This one told me to destroy you and
take over your life."

"Well, that is a VERY unpleasant thing for you
to do!" I said. "And here I was, worrying you were
more likeable than me!"

"What did this adult look like?" asked Valerie.

Georgina waved at the ingredients the clone
had gathered. "And what does the spell do?" she
demanded.

The clone looked me dead in the eye.

It destroys whoever made me.

GULP

I ordered my deadly (though still handsome) clone to stop performing the spell, but it refused.

"The adult told me not to stop, even if anyone asked me to," it said, reaching over to me and plucking a hair from my head.

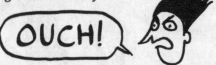

OUCH!

We huddled away from the clone to decide on a course of action. Well, Valerie and Georgina did. I was focused on nursing my sore scalp.

"Perhaps we could distract it with another task?" asked Valerie.

"That wouldn't solve the problem permanently though," said Georgina. Then her eyes lit up. "But it *has* given me an idea. I'll explain later, but we need to give it lots of instructions – quickly! Like this..."

Bake me a cake.

The clone stopped what it was doing and started walking towards the school kitchen.

Play the recorder, to grade 8 standard.

It stopped walking towards the school kitchen and started walking towards the music room. I realized what Georgina was doing.

"Eat a poo!" I commanded.

It started off towards the toilets, when I gave it another instruction.

Run around the building wearing your pants on your head!

82

As we yelled our orders faster and faster, the clone went from being stuck frozen to the spot to spinning around.

"Keep going!" yelled Georgina.

Just as I ordered, "Slap yourself in the face!" at the same time Valerie told it to, "Cuddle a puppy!" it spun so fast that it flew into the air, sparking and smoking, until—

It turned into a magical cloud and floated away!

> I did not know that you were an adept sorcerer!

"I'm not. Lunchtime is almost over, we need to get to our classrooms," said Georgina. "I'll explain on the way."

> I realized the clone was behaving just like a computer. And if you flood a computer with lots of different instructions, it can't handle it.

"I wasn't sure if it would work – this is magic, not coding – but I thought it was worth trying," said Georgina. She held her hands aloft in a gesture of victory.

> I did that!

Now, I wouldn't ordinarily acknowledge the accomplishments of others except under extreme duress, such as

84

thumbscrews. But, given that Georgina had just saved me from a killer clone, I thought perhaps I would make an exception.

"You were not *not* un-wrong," I admitted.

"Why are you like this, Loki?" said Georgina.

"There can be no logical explanation for my magnificence," I said. "It defies all explanation."

As Georgina went off to join her class, I heard her muttering:

Is it too late to swap him for the evil Killer clone?

Valerie and I, meanwhile, arrived at our classroom to find a fresh tragedy had occurred.

You're not getting me like you did the other day. I suspect this is not a TRUE tragedy. !

It is, I swear! A horrifying catastrophe! The worst of all possible outcomes!

Hmm. I am sceptical. !

Our teacher, it transpired, was ill...

! Well now I feel bad.

... which meant we had a Maths test instead of our normal lessons!

THE HORROR!

! I knew you were just being dramatic.

Dramatic? There were FRACTIONS!

On the plus side, we had takeaway for tea tonight.

On the minus side...

Can anyone explain why this was open on Loki's bedside table at the "Create a shadow self" page?

Erm...

Spells

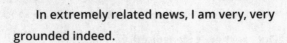

In extremely related news, I am very, very grounded indeed.

But fear not! I shall be back with more fabulously handsome adventures VERY soon...

Insult generator

One of the things I miss most about Asgard is the flyting: a battle which uses insults instead of violence. So, out of nostalgia, I have designed a flyting generator to insult each and every one of you.

First letter of your first name

A	toothless	N	pigeon-licking
B	thieving	O	massive
C	bumbling	P	horse-breathed
D	bum-sniffing	Q	cheese-kissing
E	witless	R	badly dressed
F	poo-eating	S	crumpet-fearing
G	snivelling	T	greasy-haired
H	chicken-hearted	U	useless
I	pestilent	V	pant-stealing
J	snot-munching	W	rambling
K	smug	X	gossiping
L	unwashed	Y	plotting
M	turgid	Z	potato-hatching

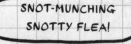

SNOT-MUNCHING
SNOTTY FLEA!

Hammer time

Inspired by my own adventures in cloning, I decided to play a trick on Thor by cloning lots of different hammers and challenging him to find Mjolnir among the mix. Can you spot it? It's the only hammer without a clone.

Are you smarter than Loki?

Below is a series of statements that are all very, very true. OR ARE THEY? Can you guess which of these very believable facts are actually facts, and which are fiction? I doubt it.

True or False?	T	F
Tuesday, the day, is named after Thor, the god.		
Freyja rides a chariot pulled by cats.		
Thor rides a chariot pulled by goats.		
Sif once cut my hair off as a joke.		
Thor farts thunder.		
I once gave birth to a seven-legged horse.		
Vikings wore horned helmets.		
Thor is my brother.		
Thor once killed a giant and used their body to make the world.		
Hyrrokkin is not actually a god, she's a giant.		

Answers

Hammer Time

This is Mjolnir a unique hammer that I tricked a dwarf into making. Mjolnir has a very short handle. That's because the dwarf got distracted when a fly bit him on the eyelid. That part has nothing to do with me.

Are you smarter than Loki?

1. **FALSE.** Actually it's named after Tyr. As Thor has his own day, Thursday, it is deeply unfair that I don't get one!

2. **TRUE.** Bit harsh on the cats if you ask me, but no one punishes her.

3. **Also TRUE.** (See above.)

4. **FALSE!** OK so it was the other way around. I cut off Sif's hair. (My identity always shifts, it's hard to remember who did what to whom when I'm so many people!)

5. **Technically TRUE.** He can do it, he just refuses to.

6. **FALSE.** Sleipnir, my pride and joy, has eight legs. It was a tough labour.

7. **FALSE.** I don't know WHERE mortals got that idea. It definitely wasn't me who started spreading the rumour to annoy and confuse historians and archaeologists. Nope, definitely not...

8. **FALSE.** Whoever started that rumour will feel my wrath.

9. **FALSE.** It was Odin who did that. (Allegedly...)

10. **TRUE.** (But I don't hold it against her.)

Acknowledgements

KAREN LAWLER... Ineffable Spouse

THE WHOLE TEAM AT WALKER... Gods of publishing

MOLLY KER HAWN... Agent of Chaos

ROBIN AND DEE... Whickber Street Puppies

GABBY HOULGRAVES... Emotional support angel

THE GIRLS... Omnipresent gods

WENDY SHAKESPEARE... Wendy the Lokist

ABBIE AND ELIZABETH... Divine Toots

RACHEL FATUROTI... God of Comics

TEAM SWAG... HORSE!

RACHEL REESE... Mythical deity

CAROLYNE LARRINGTON... Odin's latest incarnation

For more about Louie Stowell go to www.louiestowell.com

Happy
World Book Day!

When you've read this book, you can keep the fun going by swapping it, talking about it with a friend, or reading it again!

What do you want to read next? Whether it's **comics**, **audiobooks**, **recipe books** or **non-fiction** you can visit your school, local library or nearest bookshop for your next read – someone will always be happy to help.

World Book Day is about changing lives through reading

When you **choose to read** in your spare time it makes you

Feel happier	**Better at reading**	**More successful**

Find your **reading superpower** by

1. **Listening to books being read aloud (or listening to audiobooks)**
2. **Having books at home**
3. **Choosing the books YOU want to read**
4. **Asking for ideas on what to read next**
5. **Making time to read**
6. **Finding ways to make reading FUN!**

I'm orange!

Book 1

LOUIE STOWELL
GOD OF ASGARD

LOKi

A BAD GOD'S GUIDE TO BEING GOOD

"Outrageously funny
... Sharp wit, ethical
dilemmas, sly mythological
references and oodles of
doodles are a recipe for
pure reading pleasure."

THE GUARDIAN

"YOU **MUST** READ THIS BOOK,
or may you get bitten on the bum by a
snake, which could totally happen."

Jamie Smart
author of Bunny vs Monkey

I'm blue!

Book 2

LOUIE STOWELL
GOD OF A

LOKi

A BAD GOD'S GUIDE TO TAKING THE BLAME

LOUIE STOWELL
GOD OF ASGARD!

LOKi

A BAD GOD'S GUIDE TO RULING THE WORLD

Book 3

I'm green!

"This bad boy's
journey is a laugh-
out-loud delight,
packed with cartoons
and footnotes,
perfect for fans
of The Wimpy Kid."

The Daily Mail